Lonnie the Loon
Learns to Call

Barbara Renner

ISBN: 978-1-63490-243-4

Lonnie the Loon and his Mom
are floating on the lake.

Lonnie is listening to all the
sounds around him.

Interesting Fact: Loons protect their young from skunks, raccoons, foxes, and snapping turtles.

He hears "Honk, Honk, Honk."

"Mom! Is that Dad calling a friend?"

"No, dear, that's a goose
calling his mate."

Lonnie hears “Quack, Quack, Quack.”

“Mom! Is that Dad warning us about danger?”

“No, dear, that’s a duck calling her four ducklings.”

Dad lands on the water after visiting a nearby lake.

Mom swims to Dad, “I think Lonnie is ready to learn how to call.”

Interesting Fact: When landing on a lake, Loons hold their wings very high over their backs so they won’t make a crash landing.

This makes Dad very proud, so he spreads his wings and runs on top of the water to Lonnie.

"Lonnie, our Loon family makes four different sounds."

Interesting Fact: Loons call just before and after sunset. Most calling takes place at night.

Lonnie's Dad *wails*, "Oooo-**Waaa**-Oo, Oooo-**Waaa**-Oo. I make this call when I want to be closer to other loons."

"That's the one you use when you want to find me!"

Use a QR Reader App to hear the Wail call.

"When I'm alarmed by an approaching boat, I use a *tremolo* call, like this, Oo**aaaa**oo, Oo**aaaa**oo, Oo**aaaa**oo, Oo**aaaa**oo."

"You sound like you're laughing, Dad."

Use a QR Reader App to hear the Tremolo call.

"I *yodel* to warn my family about danger and to defend my home. Only Daddy Loons yodel, and it sounds like this, **aa**-wu-**waaaa**; **aa**-wu-**waaaa**; **aa**-wu-**waaaa**."

"That's the sound you make when an eagle flies over our nest.

Use a QR Reader App to hear the Yodel call.

"When our family is together, or
when we socialize with other Loons,
we *hoot*, like this, Hoo, Hoo, Hoo."

"I can make that sound when
I'm with my friends."

Lonnie swims by his Mom to practice
the calls his Dad taught him.

Use a QR Reader App to hear the Hoot call.

Listen, Mom, I can *wail*, "Oooo-
Waaa-Oo, Oooo-**Waaa**-Oo."

Listen, Mom, I can make a *tremolo*
call, "Oo**aaaa**oo, Oo**aaaa**oo,
Oo**aaaa**oo, Oo**aaaa**oo."

Listen, Mom, I can *yodel*, "**aa**-wu-
waaaa; **aa**-wu-**waaaa**; **aa**-wu-**waaaa**."

Listen, Mom, I can *hoot*,
"Hoo, Hoo, Hoo."

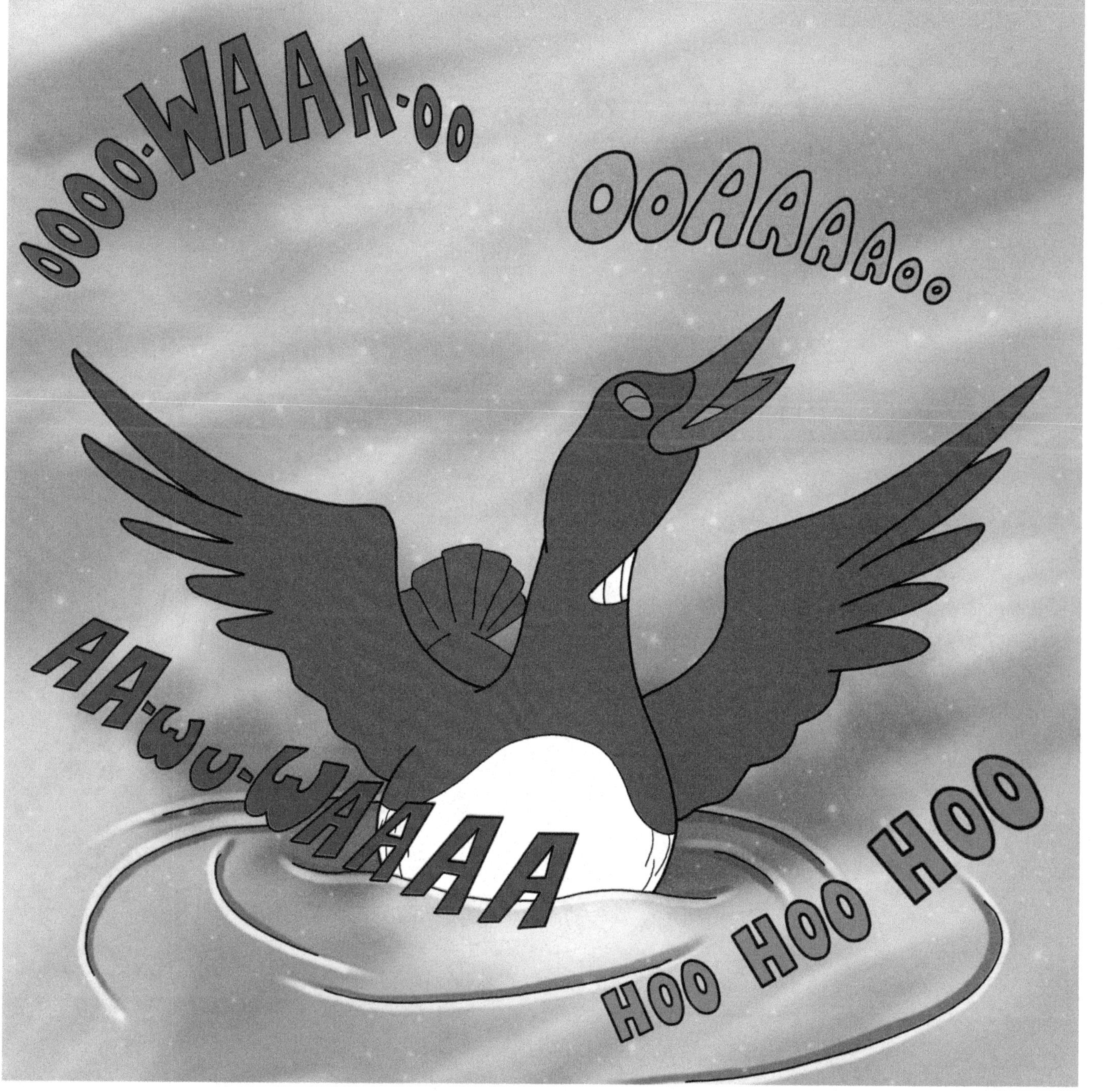

OOOO-WAAA-OO
OOAAAA..
AA-WU-WAAAAA
HOO HOO HOO

"I'm proud of you, Lonnie! You have learned all your calls."

Lonnie is happy he has learned how to call.

Interesting Fact: Loons who spend the winter along the coastal waters do not make these beautiful calls.

Oooo-**Waaa**-Oo, Oooo-**Waaa**-Oo

RESOURCES

Renner, Brian
Brian Renner Consulting
www.brianrenner.com

Tekiela, Stan
Fascinating Loons
Copyright 2006
Adventure Publications, Inc.
Cambridge, MN

The Cornell Lab of Ornithology
All About Birds; Common Loon
Website, November 23, 2014
http://www.allaboutbirds.org/guide/Common_Loon/sounds

The Loon Preservation Committee
The Voice of the Loon
Website, November 23, 2014
http://www.loon.org/voice-loon.php

CPSIA information can be obtained
at www.ICGtesting.com
Printed in the USA
LVOW06s2112140816
500372LV00004B/17/P

9 781634 902434